TO VICTORIA.
DON'T EVER STOP PAINTING YOUR DREAMS IN COLOURS.

Made with love by the team at

FIVE MILE

Five Mile,
the publishing division
of Regency Media
www.fivemile.com.au

Text, Illustrations & Cover Design © Consuela F. Ortiz

Printed in China 5 4 3 2 1

NATIONAL LIBRARY OF AUSTRALIA

A catalogue record for this book is available from the National Library of Australia

EASTER DISASTER

CONSUELO F. ORTIZ

Easter is just around the corner, and in his cosy burrow, Easter Bunny starts getting things ready. "Right-o," he says, "time to sort out those eggs!"

Shopping list
- paint (different colours)
shovel
- chocolate
lollies
- a lot of eggs
To Do
- clean brushes
- pay Rabbit Society Fee
- sweep burrow

Easter Bunny hops into town to gather everything he needs for the big day.

Paint, chocolates, and lots and lots of eggs...
the shopping list is complete!
"Let's head home!"

Once home, Easter Bunny enjoys a relaxing bubble bath.
"Ahh, this is just what I needed!" he says, sinking into the bubbly water.

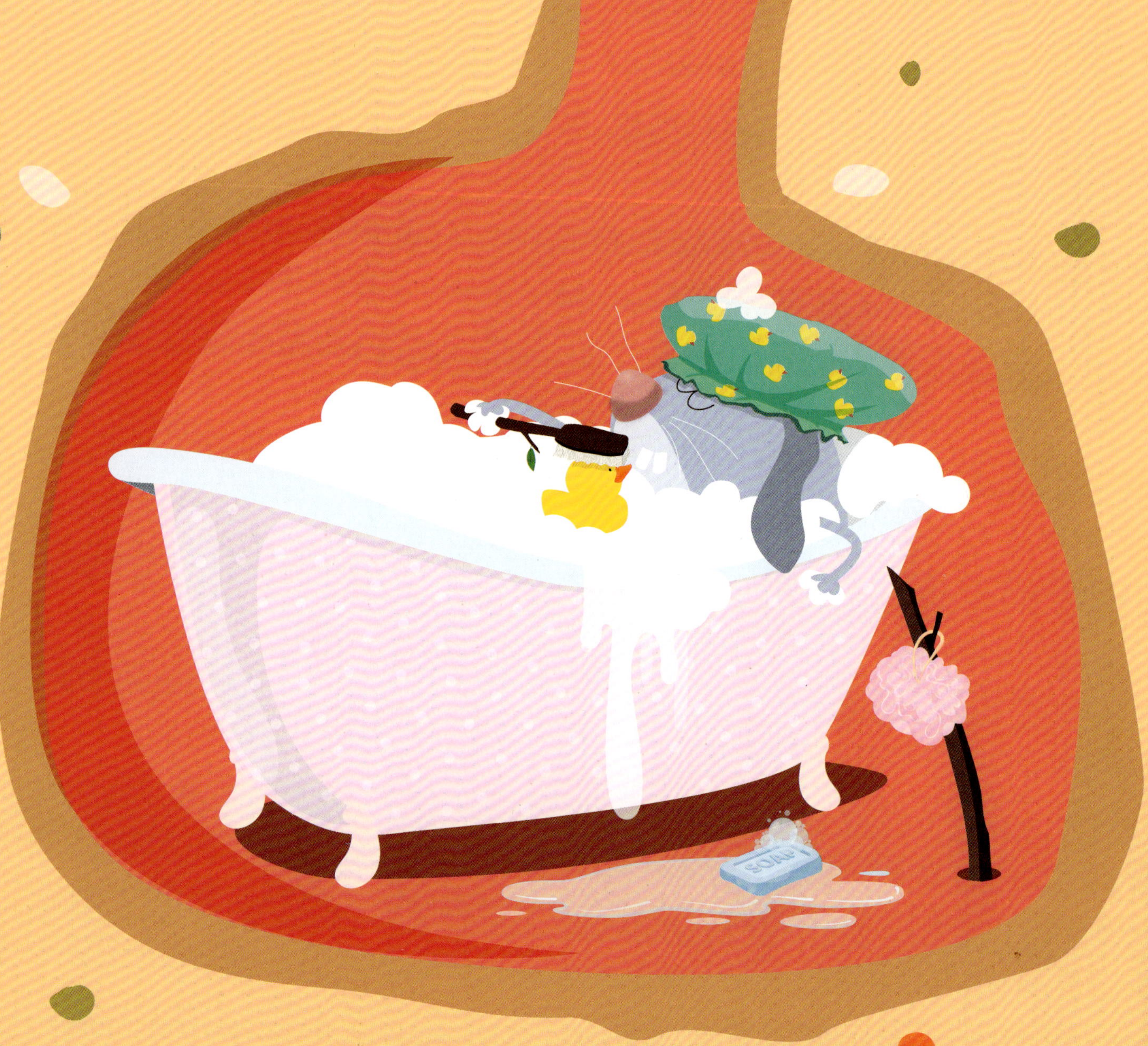

After a while, he steps out of the tub. But oh no! He slips on some soap and lands right on his paw.

"ouch! That hurts! I think I've broken it!" he cries.

Sure enough,
his paw is hurt.
"This is trouble",
he murmurs.
"I need help, and fast!
Easter can't wait!"

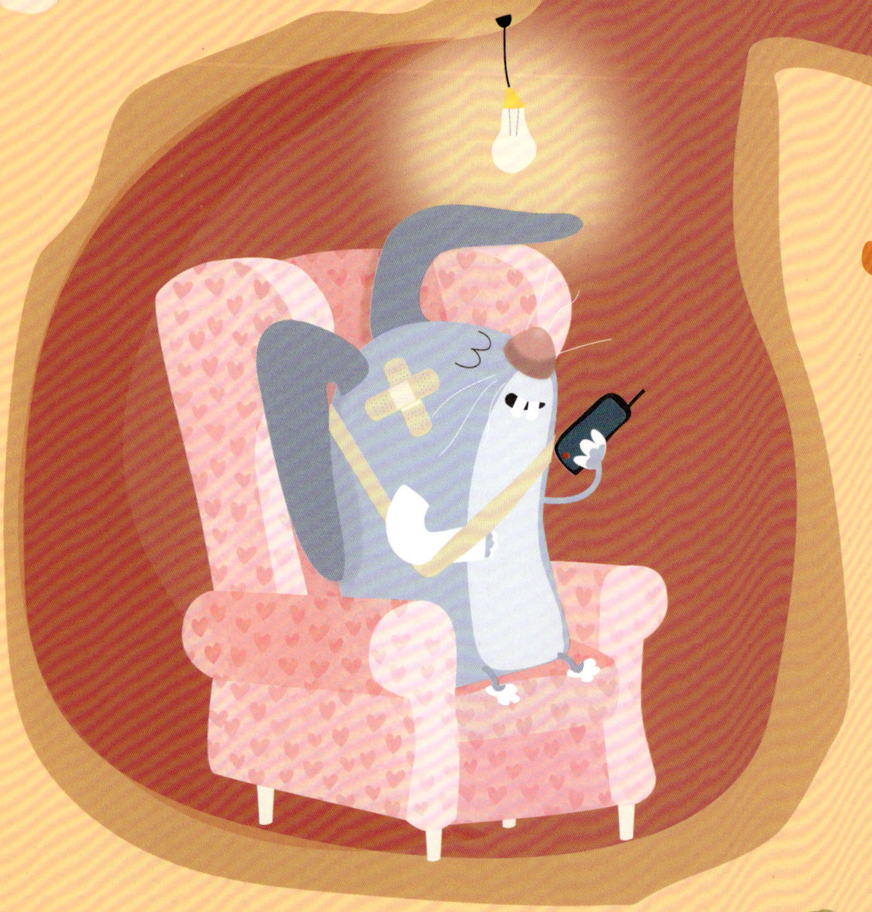

"I know, I'll call my
friends. They've never
painted or hidden eggs
before, but with a few
instructions, I'm sure
they'll do just fine!"

In a burrow not too far away, a Wombat is sleeping cosily when the phone rings. "Hello? Wombert speaking". he says.

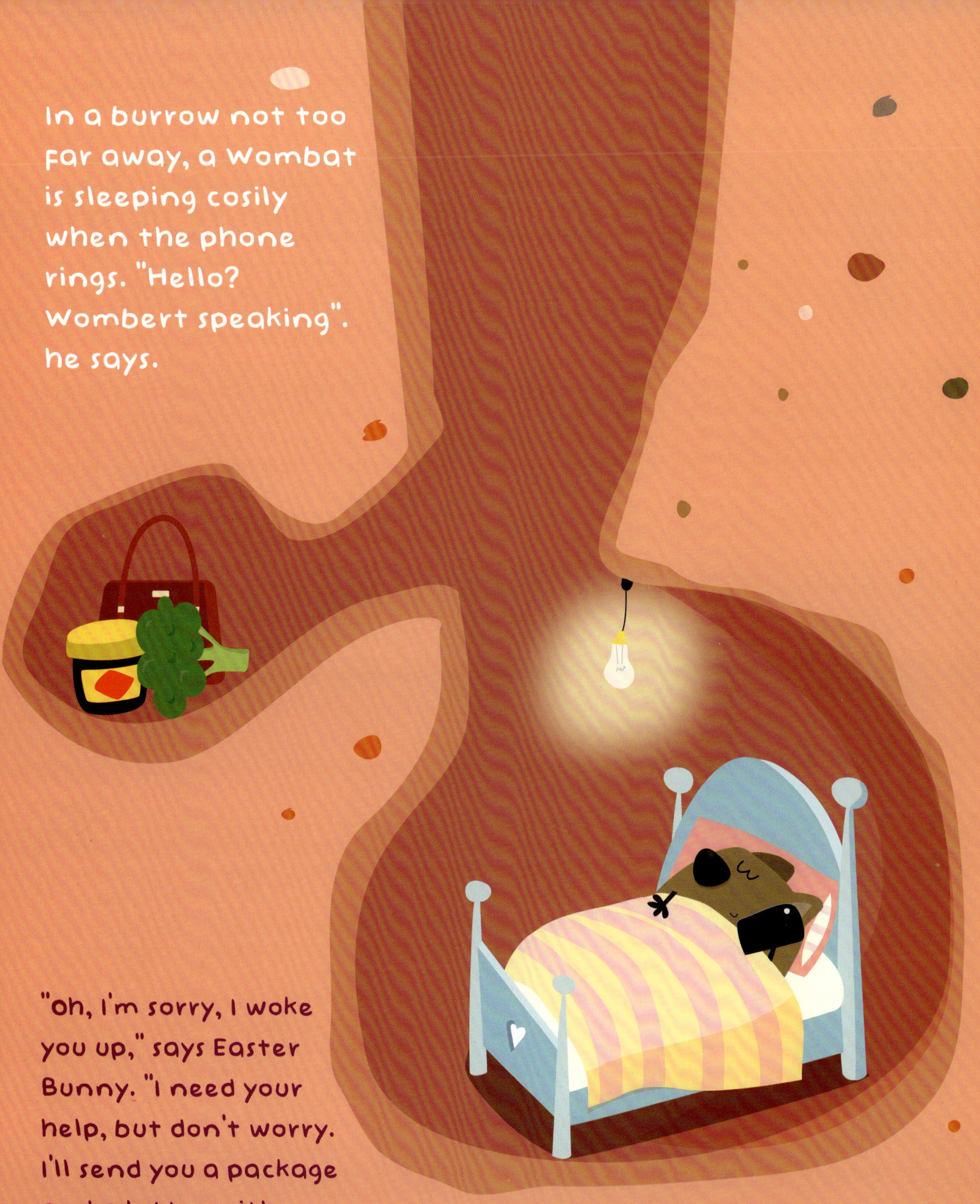

"Oh, I'm sorry, I woke you up," says Easter Bunny. "I need your help, but don't worry. I'll send you a package and a letter with instructions."

The next day, the package arrives.

Dear Friends,

Thanks for helping me this Easter!

I know you'll do a great job!

Here's what you need to do:

Put on the costumes.

Paint the eggs bright and colourful.

Hide them using the map.

Have fun!

Good luck and Happy Easter!

X X Bunny

Aussie the koala quickly tries on his bunny costume.
" Ha! It fits perfectly!" he laughs. "I love these giant ears".
This is going to be so much fun!"

"My costume fits quite tight,"
said Wombert.
"But it's fine... I can still move!"

"Hey Aussie, we look like bunnies!
Before we paint the eggs, let's munch some carrots, like real bunnies do!"

"Oh, they're super crunchy!
But I still prefer eucalyptus leaves."

PAINTING TIME...
Wombert dips his brush into the paint,
but oh no! He bumps the tin. Splat!
Blue paint goes everywhere, on his paws,
on the floor... even on his nose!
"Oops, this is harder than I thought!"

Despite their best efforts, it doesn't seem like anyone really knows what they're doing.

"Are we supposed to paint the eggs before or after hiding them?" asks Aussie, while covering the floor in fresh paint.

Just when everything feels like a big, messy disaster,
Easter Bunny hops in to check on his friends.
There's paint everywhere, broken eggs, and his helpers
are all tired and covered in colourful splashes.
"You're the silliest bunnies I've ever seen!
What a clumsy crew I have!" he laughs.

No worries! Easter Bunny's paw is on the mend, and despite the cast, he's ready to take charge and get everything back on track.

"Let's get Easter sorted!" he cheers,
hopping into action.
"Make way, bunny on a mission!"

In the end, everything turned
out just as planned.
What fun it was to hunt for
the eggs, and what a pile of
treats they found!
"It´s been an amazing day!"
they all cheered.

Maybe a little mess
is what makes Easter
fun after all!